The Boy Who Didn't Like to Eat His Mamma's Food

Paulo Ronez

Zeta Publishing

Ocala, FL

Zeta Publishing, Inc
3850 SE 58th Ave
Ocala, FL 34480
www.zetapublishing.com

This is a work of fiction. All of the characters, names, incidents, organizations, and dialogue in this novel are either the products of the author's imagination or are used fictitiously.

Ordering Information:
Quantity sales. Special discounts are available on quantity purchases by corporations, associations, and others. For details, contact the publisher at the address above.
Orders by U.S. trade bookstores and wholesalers. Please contact Zeta Publishing: Tel: (352) 694-2553; Fax: (352) 694-1791 or visit www.zetapublishing.com

Rev. Date: March 2018

ISBN: 978-1-947191-70-9 (sc)
ISBN: 978-1-947191-71-6 (e)

Library of Congress: 2018937525
Printed in the United States of America

My name is Paulo Ronez. I am writing this story because I remember when I was a child, how much I liked to hear stories. Some history are beautiful and very pleasurable to hear, but not all the histories are true. Even so, we always like to hear them, and sometimes we can learn somethings good from them. As I learned, but is not just only good to learn, but it can also bring a peace of mind. My history it's about Little Mario, a boy who learned to eat his mamma's food in a beautiful dream.

CHAPTER 1

Little Mario Home

Little Mario didn't like to eat his mamma's cooking. Little Mario is white, and he is a very intelligent boy.

The illustration in this history book was drawn by

Paulo Ronez

Little Mario home

This history it's about a boy who learn to eat his mamma's food and became strong and one of the best athletic in the high school. He always won the most contest, and he was selected to compete in the International Olympic Games.

And how he became so strong? I will tell you. His name was Mario and because his father have the same name, people call him Little Mario. And Little Mario was a very intelligent boy, and obedient boy. He have a sister older than he. Her name was Gena. They lived in a beautiful ranch where they had some livestock. Little Mario was always around his father in the ranch helping him, and asking everything about the ranch, because he liked all those animals and birds and everything in the ranch. His mother Mrs. Mary she was one of the best lady. In the church she sang all the most beautiful song, because she had a beautiful soprano voice. And there was a very happy family, even the dog, his name was Rock a very intelligent Golden Retriever dog, which loved very much Little Mario. Little Mario Father just brought all the goods from the ranch to the local markets for sale. Because they lived from those goods.

Every thing was fine with the family, except with a problem with Little Mario. Little Mario was always complaining about the food. He just eat a little and saying, I am not hungry today. His sister Gena yelled and scolded him. She said, How are you going to be strong like those boys in the school if you don't eat? They are talking about wanting to be a football players when they grow up: Look at you, You are skinny. How are you going to be strong boy like those boys in the school. Gena loved her brother very much, and she wanted see her brother strong like those boys in the school.

Gena eat very well, and couldn't understand why Little Mario didn't liked his mamma's cooking. His parents scolded him, and insisted him for eat. He eat very little and said, "I am not hungry today" and he walked to his room followed Rock the dog. His parents never spanked them for any bad behavior, because they believe the children must be educated and learn the good manners in a very polite way.

SHE SAID I COOK THE
BEST FOOD

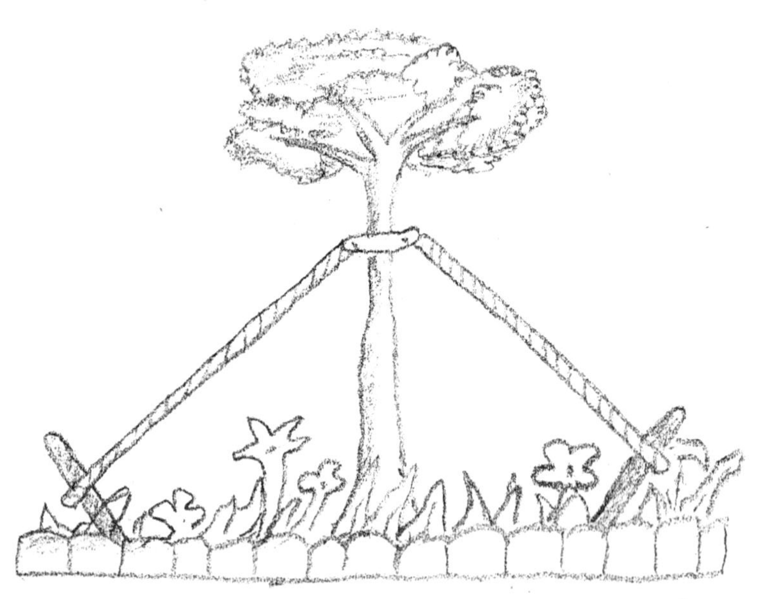

SO THAT TREE GROW STRAIGHT AND BEAUTIFUL

Mr. Mario saw his wife, she was very angry about Little Mario behavior. She said I cook the best food and he don't eat whats matter with his boy. Mr. Mario hugged his wife, and said my dear don't be angry. Lets give more time and you will see Little Mario will change his behavior.

Mr. Mario was a very religious men with great fate in "God", and he know that Little Mario will change his behavior.

He told his wife, the children like a young tree in a beautiful garden. You see when they plant a young tree, they tie up with rope that tree, so that tree grow up straight and beautiful, so we are the rope for our children to teach and bring them straight up, and they can be a rope for the other children. Next morning Mrs. Mary made a good breakfast as usual, then she went to Little Mario room to wake him up, and prepare him for school. She gave him a hug and kiss and said, I made very nice pancake go to eat, your sister she is already eating.

Little Mario sat at the table, he looked the pancake, and said I am not hungry today, I don't want eat.

His sister yelled at him and said, "You have to eat Little Mario, mamma made the best breakfast for us, and you don't eat, shame on you. Gena looked at her mamma and said, "Mom put some extra pancakes in the lunch box, and I will give to him in the break time in the school."

Mrs. Mary blessed her daughter saying "every person should be like you, caring for each other".

Don't worry my dear I will give the leftover for those beautiful animals and birds out there in the woods, because they are part of our life and they are also a creation of God, and all them deserve all the protection and love from us people.

Gena ask her mam. Why many people mistreat those innocent animals? Mrs. Mary looked at her daughter and said. "I can see you want to know why? There is no time to explain to you now. I will tell you when you come back from school." Mrs. Mary prepared the lunch box for them and said. "Go in peace and don't worry about the left over". As they were walking to take the school bus, Gena was very

angry and scolded Little Mario for not eating and making their mother very sad. Little Mario said, "Gena don't worry. Mamma can give that food for the birds and animals in the woods."

Gena scolded him again and said. "Mama doesn't cook for the animals Little Mario answered, that mama always says, we should treat the animals and birds well because they are also a creation of God like we are "When they came from school, Mrs. Mary had already prepared the lunch for them, and she said. I'll explain to both of you why some people mistreat those animals, and we should forgive them for their bad behavior" As the kids were eating their lunch, Mrs. Mary told them. We are different from each other. We are still in a stage of development and some people want to show their ability, their power and action and their uncontrolled anger. In their rage, they beat those innocent creatures by hurting them very badly. Unfortunately those defenseless and unprotected creatures are the victims of those people.

We have to understand their bad behavior and forgive them because they don't enough knowledge and love.

I ask both of you never mistreat those beautiful animals, but protect and love them.

CHAPTER 2

Little Mario Had a Dream

In his dream he was walking in the woods very hungry, and he saw a beautiful cottage.

Both kids listened to what their mother told them, and praised her for what she said. But next day was the same thing. Little Mario refused to eat saying. "I am not hungry today." His mamma became very sad and even cried. Once she even took cooking classes. She did everything to make her family happy, but Little Mario was always the same. Gena yelled and scolded him. She said "How are you going to be strong like those boys in the school? Shame on you my little brother. At the dinner time Little Mario, he eat just a little, and said "I am not hungry" and he shrunk his shoulders and walked to his room with Rock, his golden retriever dog. Rock was a beautiful, and intelligent dog. He seemed to understand the situation He just laid down close to Little Mario watching him do his homework. While he was doing his home work, Little Mario fell sleep. Then his mom came in and took him and put him his bed. She covered him and walked away closing the door in a very gentle way so as not to awake him. But something happened that night.

Little Mario had a dream. In his dream, he was walking in the woods, very hungry, looking for the way to go home, and while walking in the woods, he saw many small animals and birds: All them looking for what they would eat. He noticed they were eating whatever they could find any thing they could eat. But in his dream, he saw a beautiful big cottage there. He walked to that cottage, and knocked on the door, and the door was open by a beautiful young lady dressed like an angel. She told him, "Come in Little Mario we were waiting for you."Little Mario ask her. "How do you know my name?" She told him, I am a fairy and I brought you here because you are hungry and I want see you eat. Little Mario walked in and saw that table full of many varieties of food, he couldn't believe what he was seeing. And he asked the fairy. Who made this wonderful food? The fairy told him. All this food was made from that beautiful lady there. Little Mario asked again. And who she is?

The fairy smiling said, there she is cooking more food for you, and I am here helping her. The fairy said. "Mrs. Mary, please turn around so your son can see who is cooking all this food for him". Mrs. Mary turned around, give him a big smile and said. "Eat my dear son, because I want see you to be strong boy, like those in the school". My dear son, I am tired and I go home now to rest. And she walked out from the cottage.

Little Mario called her, Mom... Mom... wait but she gone.

The fairy told him. Little Mario your mom went home because she is very tired, and she need a good rest. And I want you eat, if you don't eat your mama food, I will be back and will take you. And the fairy disappeared throughout a big open window. Little Mario was still scared for what was happening, and he was still hungry, he try to take a piece of a baked fish, but a bobcat came in from the woods jumped on the table, and grab that fish and run away. Little Mario yelled at him saying "Stop... stop... this fish my mom cooked for me, but the bobcat got away with that fish. Little Mario try to take a piece of cake, then a big bunch of birds flush in, and got away with that cake. He yelled again. "Stop... stop... and said this cake my mom did for me. But this time, a big bunch of squirrels jump on the table

followed by birds and some other smalls animals, and all them were very hungry, they started to eat all the foods. Little Mario jumped up and started to yell again "Stop... stop... to eat this food because my mom did for me, and continued yelling to them very loudly. "Stop... stop... But this time his mom run to his room, and saw Little Mario seating on his bed very scared. Mrs. Mary gave him a hug, and kiss and said. You just had a bad dream my son. Go eat your breakfast, your sister she is already eating. After Little Mario clean himself and dressed up he went to the kitchen where his sister was already eating, he seat down close to her, and was thinking about his bad dream, but not eating. Gena asked him; Why you don't eat? He told her. Sis I had a terrible dream, and I am still shaking. Gena looked at him and said, we all have some times bad dream, but this is not the reason for you not eat. Little Mario just eat a little, He looked at the pancakes and said, "I don't want eat, I am not hungry".

His sister yelled at him and said. "You have to eat Little Mario, mamma made the best breakfast for us and you don't eat" Shame on you". Gena looked at her mom and asked her again. "Mama put some extra pancakes in my lunch box, and I will give to him at the break time in the school".

Mrs. Mary she had already prepared the lunch box for them and said. "Go in peace, and don't worry about the left over of food." As they were walking to take the school bus, Gena she was angry and scolded him again for not eating and making their mother very sad. Little Mario said. "Gena don't worry, mamma can give that, for the birds and animals in the woods."

CHAPER 3

Little Mario Had Another Dream

How wonderful is to fly. Little Mario save those geese from a big disaster.

When they came back from the school, their mother she already had prepared the lunch for both. Little Mario just eat a little and went to help his father on the ranch, as he always did, because he loved the life in the ranch. At the dinner time his father made the Prayer as usual, he thanks Gods for the wonderful day they had, and thanks for the daily food. Little Mario just eat a little and said, "I am not very hungry, and asked excuse, and went to his room to do his homework, followed by Rock, the very friendly dog. But that night Little Mario had another dream. This time the dream was different.

The beautiful fairy flew into his room like a big eagle and stood on his bed. Little Mario jumped and said, "You again" She looked at him smiling and said "Remember what I told you last time? I will come here if you don't eat your mama's cooking.

Now I will take you for another trip. You are going to be an eagle. Look at your body covered with feathers, also your arms have two beautiful wings. Now Little Mario, you are an eagle like me and you will fly with me. Little Mario asked, "how can you become an eagle if you were a lady?" The fairy smiled at him and said, "I can be anything as long as I am doing things right and doing good for all the People. Now Little Mario, you will fly with me. The boy asked where they were going. We are going to see more eagles like us. Little Mario said "How wonderful is to fly. I wish I could be an eagle" After a long fly, Little Mario saw something very interesting. He saw a bunch of geese flying and singing making a "V" shape. He saw one bird in the front leading all the other birds in "V" shape. He asked the fairy why those birds flying in a "V" shape? She answered it's so this way they can cut off the wind and make their flight easier. "Very interesting" Little Mario said. But he noticed something was going wrong. He told the fairy and showed her the big airport a few miles ahead. He told her those birds could be killed because they are flying in that direction. They can be sucked into the engine of those big jumbo jet airplanes and there can be a big disaster. Little Mario asked her. "Please lets do something before that happens" The fairy looked at Little Mario and asked" "What can we do? Little Mario remembered what his mother said "Love and protect them." Little Mario replied, "Let me fly in front of them so that way I can move them away from the airport. The fairy realized Little Mario was really concerned and wanted to save the life of those geese. She said, "Is this because you want to obey your mama?" Little Mario got angry and said, "I want to save the life of those birds because I love them and they deserve protection from us" You are an eagle and those geese won't follow an eagle" Little Mario insisted, and told her, "You made me an eagle, now let me be a goose than I can lead them away from the airport". The fairy turned him into a big singing Goose. Little Mario flew right way to the front of the "V" and directed the geese far from the airport. The fairy turned Little Mario back to an eagle again, and those geese were very surprised to follow a strange goose. Then the new leader of the geese took over the "V" and flew them south. All the geese

looked and saw that big goose that flew them away from the airport was that big eagle. They couldn't understand what happened.

CHAPTER 4

A eagle catch a big fish to feed their baby. Little Mario us a eagle he save those birds from a big snake.

The eagle catching a fish in the big lake

Little Mario and the fairy continued their flight until they stopped on top of a big tree. Little Mario stopped close to her and asked why those geese were flying south. She told him because in the south, it's much easier to find food than in the north due to the cold of the winter. Little Mario didn't say any thing, but understood how wonderful it would be to be eating his mother delicious food. The fairy then showed him a nest where a mama eagle was feeding her baby with a dead rat that she caught in the field. The fairy showed it to Little Mario, another eagle that was flying over a big lake. She said "Let's go down there an see what that eagle is doing in the lake". The eagle was a strong bird of pray. He has a very sharp eyesight. He was flying close to the water that way he could catch a fish and then bring it to feed the baby. Little Mario said. "The baby eagle is eating the raw fish." I won't eat raw because mama fries the best fish which I could eat all of the time". Little Mario looked at the fairy said. "No I don't want to be an eagle eating raw fish, and dead rats, no not me". The fairy told him. "Lets go down in to the field.

By this time, Little Mario was hungry asking for food. The fairy told him, "You don't want to be an eagle eating raw fish? Then you can be a bird eating wild berries". The boy turned into a bird, and started to eat berries, but the berries were sour and some were even bitter. He could not eat any more, and he started to cry saying, "I want to go home and eat my mama's wonderful cooking. The fairy looked at him and said. "Little Mario you just started to see how these wonderful creatures live. She called his attention to look over at that snake. It's going up on that tree, trying to catch that bird to eat. Come Little Mario, fly with me, and you will see many more beautiful living creatures we have in this wonderful planet created by our Creator Little Mario asked her, who is this creator you talk about, my mama always talked about this creator." He is God" The fairy said. "Now let's fly on top of that tree" Little Mario replied, "I want to be a big eagle again". So that fairy turned Little Mario to a big eagle. She said now you come fly with me" Little Mario said, no, first I want to save that bird from the snake which was very close to the nest. But the fairy warned him about the danger because that snake was big could kill him. Little Mario didn't pay attention and flew to that tree. He saw the big snake very close to the bird's nest ready to catch the bird. Then Little Mario remembered the technique. He flew with his open sharp claw, curved nails, and grabbed the big snake. He flew high and the fairy was flying close to him yelling to drop the snake. But Little Mario said, "I want to take this snake far away from here so it won't come back to catch this birds again. The fairy kept yelling, fly high over that hill, and drop that snake on the rocks. The fairy saw that Little Mario was changing his behavior for good. But he still was hungry and wanted to eat. The fairy told him, "let's fly away from here" While they were flying, Little Mario pointed out to the

fairy, Look down there, it's my home and there is my mama. She is throwing away that food which I didn't eat. I will go down there and eat that food". The fairy said, "That is the food which you said your mama can throw in the woods for the wildlife.

CHAPTER 5

Little Mario as a eagle eating his mamma's food in the woods. He said my mama food is the best even in the woods. The fairy told him, I'll explain to you about our creator which your mamma always talk about.

LITTLE MARIO
AS A EAGLE EATING HIS
MAMMAS FOOD IN THE WOODS

Then he went down and started to eat. While he was eating, Rock the dog, was watching and wagging his tail very close to that eagle. Mrs. Mary looked at rock and said, Rock looks like you know that eagle. But that eagle was Little Mario. After he finished eating, he flew away and said to the fairy, "my mama's food is the best even in the woods." The fairy told him, "let's fly on top of that tree close to the river, and I'll explain to you something about our Creator which your mama always talk about. Look at this beautiful blue sky. If we could fly in this endless Universe, we could see, many beautiful planets like ours that was created by our Supreme Being, The God which your mama talks about. Little Mario said "but I don't see anything. "The fairy answered, "You can't see the creator, but you can see what He created for us. "Little Mario said, What he created for us? The fairy answered, "look for those beautiful birds singing: Every one singing different from each other. Look down the river, you can see those big fish which can supply our need for food. Look at those squirrels running around looking for anything they can eat. "Then the fairy said, "Little Mario, we could go around in this planet and find everything we need to live, even in the big jungle those creatures find food. This planet is our home: is the mansion of our creator. "Little Mario was so interested in what the fairy was telling him, he asked why so many people in this planet have starvation? The fairy said. "It's because we are in one stage of learning how to control our living. In some places, we have an abundance for what we need and you should thank the Creator because you were born in a wonderful place where you have many things to keep you alive. Now you know why your mamma prays and thanks God for everything you have. You should listen when she talks to you, because when parents talks to their kids, they don't just talk, but they are teaching their kids. That's why there are many intelligent kids today, because they listened and obey their parents.

Little Mario asked the fairy, "Do you think God will punish me because I didn't eat my mamma's food? "No Little Mario, God didn't create people to punish them, God give the intelligence for the people to make things right. If you make things wrong, you are punishing yourself, God is with you waiting for you to be a wonderful person. Little Mario said "From now on I will try to be good" The fairy told him. For you to be good, You must be honest. Never lie, obey your parents, and love all the people around you. Help them as much as you can, and you will be loved by everyone and rewarded by God. That is the secret of God: The secret of our creator is endless."

Little Mario asked the fairy. "How do I know if God is helping because I never saw God? The fairy said "You don't see God, but God see you twenty four hours a day and every minute because God lives in you. And God is not just in us, but he also gives the power for us to do wonderful things. He gives to scientists the power and the intelligence to explore the new methods of growing wheat, which is good for our lives. And just look at those astronomers, how enthusiastic they are explore the universe those regions that are unknown to find out more about the universe. It's because they have the Aura of God surrounding them.

CHAPTER 6

Little Mario save the mama rabbit from a big snake.

Little Mario asked the fairy; What is this aura you talk about because I don't see and feel anything around me?" The fairy said: "Little Mario I know it's a little complicated for you to understand what is this aura. It's the atmosphere of spiritualism that surrounds us created from God since we are born. Try always to be honest and good all the time, because this aura will protect you from many problems. People who are dishonest, tend to lie, cheat or steal, they are losing this aura, that is the power of God. They end up even in prison, because they were very close to the devil And I don't want this to happen to you."

Little Mario asked. "Please let me fly like those big eagles. How wonderful is to fly. I wish I could be an eagle if I didn't have to eat those rats. "He was flying up and down close to the ground. Suddenly, he saw a snake trying to catch a mama rabbit, who was protecting her babies. Little Mario flew down close to the ground to catch the snake, but he missed that catch. The fairy yelled to him. You can be killed by that snake, but Little Mario wouldn't give up. He try again. This time he came very close to the snake. He took a very good look at how big the snake was and he remembered something from the first time when he saw the eagle catch a big fish. Little Mario use the same tactics again. He flew down, with open legs and open claws coming very close to the snake and grabbed the snake head then started to fly away. The fairy was yelling, "don't drop the snake keep flying up and follow me over that hill." When they were very high up she said, "now you can drop the snake" They continued their flight home.

CHAPTER 7

The fairy and Little Mario were flying over the big lake, they saw a lady with some kids in a boat she was struggling to keep the boat from a big water fall.

The fairy looked at him and said "You saved the lives of those baby rabbit, and I am feeling very proud of you" But Little Mario was scared, thinking He could be killed by that big snake. He didn't even look down any more. He felt proud for what he did. The fairy told him, "We have to fly up on this river until we reach that big lake where you saw those eagles catching those big fish, and from there we can see your home." As they were flying the fairy said, Look down there Little Mario, you can see that big water fall over those rocks. "Little Mario said "Yes and I also can see the fish jumping and trying to go upstream in the river. Little Mario asked "Why didn't the eagles from the big lake came down here to catch the fish?" The fairy answered him, It's because it's very dangerous and they can be killed on those rocks." Little Mario saw something else: He saw a boat with some kids in it. And also there was a lady with them. He saw the lady struggling to keep the boat out of the stream which was dragging the boat to the water fall. The paddle which she was using slipped out of her hands and it was going straight to the water fall. She try to grab the paddle, but the boat turned over and all the boys and the lady fell in the water. Little Mario saw something he could not believe, he saw one of the boys was a dark boy, and he was made from wood. He was yelling to them to grab his body, because he didn't sink. But Little Mario wanted to save the others. He asked the fairy to turn him into human so he could go down in the river and helped them. "No I can't do this for you Little Mario because you are too weak as a human. That's why your mama kept telling you to eat and be strong like your father." But Little Mario wouldn't give up his courage to save those kids he saw their little dog running on the river side barking to them. The little dog jumped into the river and swam to the paddle, trying to bring it to the lady. She was far away from the kids, hanging on that boy made of dark wood. But Little Mario couldn't wait any longer and he flew down to the river with open claws, grabbing the paddle, with the little dog still holding on to it.

Little Mario brought the paddle to the lady and she swam to the kids. Then the kids grabbed the paddle, and the wood boy yelled to them, let go of the boat because it's pulling us to the river stream. Then he rescued the boys taking out of the river. When they were out of the river, they looked up to the sky and with very happy hearts said. "Thank you, thank you good Lord. You sent an angel from above to save us. Thank you good Lord but his angel was Little Mario and the fairy continued flying around a few more times. The little dog was running around those kids very happy to see them. Little Mario asked the fairy, "who is that lady there with all those kids? "The fairy said she is a teacher and she brought her students camping, and all the other kids are up there. She puts only five kids in the boat at a time. But this time, she came very close in the water stream and she lost control of the boat. That's what happened." Little Mario asked the fairy "Who is that dark boy made from wood and where did he came from?" She told him is father is a lumber jack

Little Mario flew down to the river very close to the water fall, grabbing the paddle with the little dog still holding on it, and he brought the to the lady in the river.

and he found a beautiful tree. It was a dark mahogany tree. His father sold part of the tree to a furniture factory, but he kept the best part of that tree for himself. He carved that boy for himself. But it doesn't matter where he came from. The most important thing is you helped him to save those kids from the big waterfall. "But I still don't understand how that boy could act like a human being, Little Mario said. the fairy just looked at Little Mario giving him a big smile and said that has to be another dream and another story. Little Mario you just think in our world we have lots of jungles and all those jungles we can find many good things. It doesn't matter the color, but also we find lots of rotten trees which are not good even to make a scarecrow. it doesn't matter which forest that boy came from.

I will tell you something Little Mario, you just listen to your to parents and obey them because I don't want to see you get lost in any jungle. Little Mario replied if I don't go in the forest or jungle, how can I be lost. The fairy told him. "I can see you don't understand which jungle I am talking about. I will explain it to you Little Mario. you must pay attention when your mama prays, and when she is asking for God to protect her two kids from any kind of abuse: to save them from drugs, from bad company. She also asked God to protect all children abused by all kind of people and to protect all children abused by those church people. Little Mario looked the fairy and said. "Now I understand what you mean about being careful and not getting in the jungle. Little Mario, "said "I am starving and I want to go home" While they were flying, the fairy told him, Little Mario remember the dark boy made from the mahogany tree who saved the lives of those kids in the river? You also go see lots of furniture made from mahogany wood, not just that boy, and just follow his example and you will grow up to be a big hero. Little Mario replied, "Yes but I don't want to be any furniture. After a good long flight, Little Mario reached his home. The fairy opened the window and Little Mario flew back to his bed. the fairy turned Little Mario back to a human again and Rock the dog, started to bark. Mrs. Mary, Little Mario mother, ran into Little Mario room. She saw Rock standing on the window still looking out and barking. Mrs. Mary walked to the window and looked out to see if she could see anything wrong. But everything was alright. So she closed the window. Then she saw two beautiful big feathers on the floor in the room. She called her husband and showed him the feathers. He looked and said. "Looks like the eagle feathers." He looked at Rock, and said, "Rock you been out there hunting?" Little Mario was sitting on his bed smiling at Rock.

CHAPTER 8

On the way to the school Little Mario ask his sister Gena, when you talk to me, or somebody else, talk slow in a clear English.

The teacher singing.
America the Beautiful.

LUNCH BOX
SIS, WHE YOU TALK
TO ME, OR SOMEBODY ELSE,
TALK SLOW, AND A CLEAR ENGLISH.

He said "mamma, I want to hug you and kiss you. Mrs. Mary gave him a hug and kiss and told him, "Go eat the pancakes I made for you and your sister, she is already eating. Little Mario started to eat the delicious pancakes on after other. His sister looked at him and said. "You're eating all the pancakes. She called her mamma and said. "Mamma Little Mario is eating all the pancakes and we don't have any to take to the school. Mrs. Mary said don't worry, I will make more. Let him eat all he wants.

From that beautiful dream Little Mario had. He learned to eat all the food that his mom was making for them. And he started to be one strong boy admired by everyone. But we don't have to have the beautiful dream like Little Mario had, because our mom she always is doing the best for us. Mrs. Mary made more pancakes and put them in their lunch boxes, and both hugged and kissed their mama. They walked to the main road and waited for the school bus. Gena was saying something that Little Mario could not understand and she yelled to him, "don't you understand what I am saying? Little Mario looked at her said. Sis, can I ask you something? Gena answered, what you want. "What I want is when you talk to me or somebody else, try to clear your English, and talk slow because I almost don't understand what you are saying. Remember mama also said this. She also said she will come to the school and ask the principal to ask all the teachers to teach all the students to talk slow and in a clear language so people will understand what they are saying. Remember how many times mama had to call daddy to the phone because she couldn't understand what people were saying because they talk too fast and they don't have a clear English. You know sis, I am very lucky because our teacher taught to talk slow so the people could understand what we are saying.

She also said when you grow up and you talk to somebody, or in a meeting, the people like to listen to you talk because you talk in a clear language. She also said, the art of talking is almost the art of singing. How nice when you listen to somebody sing in a beautiful voice. It open your heart to love and live in peace more closely to God. You know sister, one little girl asked her to sing something for us, she gave

The teacher singing
America the beautiful

a beautiful smile for that girl, and said. "yes, I can see that you are waiting for me to sing something beautiful for you all." The kids jumped up and said. "Yes teacher sing something for us." She said o.k., I will sing and you all will sing with me." She sang and we all followed what she sang. She had a beautiful voice. Gena asked what she sang. Little Mario said, "She sang that beautiful song which daddy always sang. America the Beautiful. When she finished, we all applauded the teacher. One girl said, "teacher you have a beautiful voice like mama when she is singing in the church." Gena asked again, Little Mario why do you want me to improve my talking? Do you think I will be a singer? Little Mario answered, "You are my sister and a I love you and I don't like those kids in the school making fun of you because you talk too fast." Gena felt a little uncomfortable for what her brother asked her, but she understood what he said it with love.

In the bus, Little Mario was sitting close to the window and kept looking up to the sky thinking about the beautiful dream he had. His sister was close to him. She was thinking about what her brother told her. Gena asked him, why are you looking up there? You can't see anything but the clouds.

CHAPTER 9

Little Mario gave the money he founded to the teacher. The teacher took Little Mario to the principal's office.

Little Mario looked at her and said, "never mind what I am looking at, mind your own business." When the bus arrived in the school, all the kids were walking across the parking lot and one kid saw something falling from the ski. He was very surprised. He said, "look something is falling from our flag." It was a big beautiful feather. The boy picked up the feather and said "look, it's an eagle feather which fell out from our flag." Little Mario gave him a big smile. As they continued walking through the parking lot, Little Mario found a five dollar bill. His sister said, "how like you are Little Mario in finding money. I never found anything." Little

Mario said, "do you think I am lucky? How would you feel losing a five dollar bill? Sister just think about the person who lost this money." Gena didn't say anything anymore. When they were in class, Little Mario stood up and told the teacher he found a five dollar bill in the parking lot and if she wanted to ask who lost this money. He gave the money to the teacher. At the same time, the boy who found that beautiful feather stood up and said, he found this feather which fell from our flag. Little Mario looked at the him and said that feather he found fell out from an eagle that symbolized a beautiful land of peace. The teacher applauded Little Mario and said he shows us that he is a very good boy. Every kid in the class applauded Little Mario for his action. Little Mario looked at his teacher and the kids and said, "To be good is not important. We must be honest first, then we can be good." The teacher took Little Mario's hand and said to go with her to the principal's office.

CHAPTER 10

Little Mario ask the principal. Sir, did you liked to eat your mamma's food when you was a little boy? The principal gave him a big smile and said.

There she explained to the principal the action the boy did. The principal looked at Little Mario and said, "I just had a phone call from a mother asking if somebody found a five dollars which she gave to her daughter to buy lunch for her and her two brothers." The principal shook Little Mario's hand and said. "Little Mario you're right, we must be honest before, then we can be good. And from now on you are a great Mario."

As Little Mario was walking out from the principal's office he stopped close to the beautiful dark mahogany desk and he remembered those words from his dream that the principal said. We must be honest before, then we can be good.

Little Mario looked back at the principal and said, "Sir, may I ask you something?"

The principal said yes. Little Mario asked him, "Did you liked to eat your mamma's food when you were a little boy?" The principal gave him a big smile, and said, "I learned to eat my mamma's food in a very hard way, in a dream." The principal said, "In my dream I saw a beautiful young girl, like an angel, she was a fairy, she jumped into my room through the window and said, 'Thomas you didn't eat your mamma's food, and you said, 'she can throw that food in the garbage, because it's cheap and it cames very ease.' Thomas, you came with me, and will show you from where that food cames.'" Thomas asked her, "How do you know my name?" The fairy told him, "I know the names of everybody that I help. Now jump out through the window and I will show you from where the food comes." When Thomas jumped out, the fairy turned him into a big strong burro, and that beautiful fairy jumped on his back and said, "Keep going on that road, and I will show you those beautiful fields where the food is coming from." Thomas was very interested to see everything, and he was running faster and faster.

On that road with the fields the fairy said stop. He stopped, and she showed him a small ranch, and there was a little boy plowing the soil and a cow pulling the plow. The cow had her baby calf close to her. And the boy was yelling to her saying, "Go tom boy go…go faster go." The cow had her baby close to her all the time. Thomas asked the fairy, "Why they named that cow Tomboy?" She told him, "because tomboy is a strong girl like a boy, and that cow she is strong like bull pulling that plow." Thomas told the fairy, "it's very interesting the cow has my name. Tom but I am not a cow." The fairy said, "let's keep going ahead there are more interesting things to show you." And after another run they finally reached a farm, and there the fairy told the farmer "I brought you this big burro, and he will help you here in the farm." The farmer said thank you very much, because our burro is old, and he can't help us very much. The farmer walked to that big burro and said, "You are strong burro, and you can help us very much." He called him helper and said, "give him water and food, and after that put the harness on him." But that burro is Thomas the boy, and he yelled to the farmer saying, "I am not a burro, I am not a

cow to pull that plow, I am a boy." But the only thing the farmer could hear was the burro saying he-haw…he-haw…he-haw, that is the burro's neigh. After they put the harness on Tom the burro, he sat down like a real burro, and he wouldn't get up. The farmer brought him some carrots and said, "get up and eat these carrots, and go to work, you have to pull this plow." But the burro did not want to get up. Then the farmer took a whip and started to hit Tom the burro because in his dream he was a strong burro, and he must pull that plow to prepare the soil for planting. After many hours of hard work, and soil was plowed and ready for planting, the farmer came and said, good job young burro, that's enough for today, and tomorrow you have to plow the other side.

The farmer told the helper release the burro and bring him to the field and there he can find nice grass to eat. Tom as a burro still yelling I am not a burro, I am a boy. But what those people just heard was that burro neighing, and he was in the field he saw that fairy, he started to cry and said to her, "Please, I want to go home." The fairy looked at him and said. "Now you saw how hard these people work to bring food to the people. The food you said to your mom to throw out in the garbage." Tom the burro boy, asked her again, please take me home, the fairy jumped on his back and said, let's go home. Tom the burro boy ran faster and faster to go home, still yelling. I am not a burro…I am not a burro, I am a boy. But this time his father and his mother ran to his room and saw Tom sitting on his bed crying and still yelling I am not a burro, I am a boy. His father hugged him and said. "You are not a burro, you are my son." That was the dream the principal had, and told Little Mario. I learned to eat my mamma's food, it was the best food in this world, I ate, and she never more had to throw out any food in the garbage.

The principal also said to the Great Little Mario "I keep telling all the children, listen to your parent's, hear what they are teaching you, and obey them, because they are the best friends you can have in this world.

As little Mario was walking out from the principal's office, he looked at the principal desk, that was a beautiful mahogany desk, that reminded him about his dream about that dark boy made from wood, that he was in the river, saving the teacher, and those kids from the big water falls.

Little Mario touched that desk and said. "You are beautiful and good whatever you are, and stay that way, because I don't want you to be a big eagle eating dead rat's or raw fish, or be a big burro eating raw carrots and pulling a plow.

And he walked out from the principal's office very happy. And from that day, they stopped to calling him, Little Mario, and he became the Great Mario. As they were going home in the school bus very happy, Gena his sister asked, "Why are you so happy?" Little Mario answered. "I'll tell you when we are at home." Soon they arrived home Little Mario ran to his mother and said. "Mom give me a hug, I want to tell you something good that happened to me today in the school." And after he

BABY BUFFALO

gave the good news to his mom, she gave him another hug and kiss, and told him, "Take your lunch and go help your daddy on the ranch."

After he finished to eat his lunch, Little Mario went to the ranch whistling very happy to give his daddy the good news. He told him what happen to him in the school. His daddy praised him, and told Little Mario. "I also have good news to tell you. One of our cows, the sweet, she will give birth any time this week." They called her sweet because she was really sweet cow, as a matter of fact, Little Mario used to jump on her back, and she carried him around on the ranch. After a few days the cow gave birth to a beautiful calf. And will became a beautiful black male steer. That left Little Mario very happy whistling all the time. And because he loved all those animals, and the life on the ranch, he asked his father if he could give a name to that beautiful black calf. His father say yes, you can. Little Mario told his father, our country has a beautiful histories about Buffalos I want to call him Buffalo, and Buffalo was raised by Little Mario full of love. And he became a very friendly bull to everyone, and also to the Great Little Mario.

This is the history of a boy, who became a hero and learned to eat his mamma's food, and was loved by everyone, and also by Buffalo who became a very friendly bull to everyone and also to the Great Little Mario.

And the end of this history show how much this bull loved people but not just the bull, because most animals show their love to other animals, and also to people.

I ask you, please never mistreat those innocent animals, but love them and treat them with love because they also love us. And talk to them in a very friendly way, and don't yell at them. Let them feel as a part of the family.

It's a blessing from "God" to have these beautiful animals and birds around us because we are all the same, a beautiful creation of our "Good Lord God".